Zarma Folktales
of Niger

D1027187

Zarma Folktales
of Niger

Translated by Amanda Cushman

Quale Press

A book is never the work of a single person, and I'd like to thank others who helped with this one. First, I would like acknowledge the friends and teachers I had in Africa, especially Laouali, who gave me this book of folktales. Next, thanks to the many who kept me sane back when this was a thesis: Jordan Awerbach, Laura Callen, Joe Gallagher, Rob Gammell, Chiyo King, and Will Lane. Translation is tricky, and a few people helped along the way: Krissy Ellsworth, Joe Maddens, and Sue Rosenfeld. My gratitude goes to Kenneth Krattenmaker and Debbie Mioduszewski for their help with the cover design, and to Gian Lombardo for seeing this as more than a thesis project. Finally, thanks to my amazing family: my parents who support everything I do (even my running off to Africa), Jeremiah who is always willing to read a page or two for me, and Nico, my personal cheerleader. I'm sure there are many more that helped me in ways I don't even know.

Contents

Introduction

THIS BOOK IS a translation of *Contes Djerma Nigérien* produced by Nouvelle Imprimerie du Niger. The text of that book is written in both French and Zarma, and this translation is from the French version. These stories come from the oral tradition of West Africa. Such tales are told by *griots*—the minstrels of the culture—at festivals and special events.[1] At home, after the sun goes down and all the work is done, elders use folklore to share their wisdom, and there exist as many variations of these tales as there have been twilights.[2] This brief collection reveals only a small hint of a rich culture.

As an undergraduate, I partook of a rare opportunity to study abroad in one of the poorest countries of the world. One of my goals for college had been to learn an African language, and what better way than to go live in an African country? In the spring of my junior year, I headed across the ocean to the sparsely populated country of Niger.

Over the four months that I lived there, I learned much about the two main cultures found in Niamey, the capital. I studied both Hausa and Zarma languages (along with French), and engaged regularly in conversation with the friendly locals.[3] I studied their cultures through classes, field work, and personal adventures like visits to markets or participating in baptisms and weddings. Wherever I went, people were eager to share their culture.

I had little contact with folklore on a personal level while I was there. I spent a week living with a Hausa family in the city, and in the evenings, after the children were done with their homework, they shared jokes and traditional short, funny stories with me. Here and there I learned a proverb, such as the Zarma saying: "*Moso moso, chorizay ga fiti cheen,*" which means "Little by little, the bird builds its nest." It is shortened to "moso moso," a phrase I heard often as I struggled to learn several languages at once.

Though I found out about these cultures by studying dance, music, and crafts (I was apprenticed to a leather maker at the National Museum), I was disappointed not to be learning more of their folklore. I was thrilled when, toward the end of my French course, my teacher, Laouali, brought a book of folktales for me to study. He presented the book to me as a gift at the end of the semester because he saw how much I enjoyed it.

There are many English translations of African folklore, but they are mainly stories from the better-known cultures, such as the Zulu or Hausa. There are also those generic collections of "Folktales of Africa" that do not lay claim to any region. There are few mentions of the Zarma people anywhere. Considering their relatively small population, this is not surprising. Between two and three million Zarma speakers live in West Africa, making up only 21 percent of Niger's population.[4] They live almost exclusively around the capital, Niamey, but extend into the neighboring countries of Mali and Benin.[5]

There are three other large ethnic groups in Niger: Fulani, Tuareg, and Hausa. The first two are semi-nomadic; the Fulani are peaceable while the Tuareg struggle to dominate the lands they consider their own. The Hausa are one of the largest ethnic groups in West Africa, and are considered the business-people of the region. The wide reach of the Hausa means that their folklore has had greater opportunity to be collected and disseminated by cultural anthropologists and folklorists from other parts of the world. However, sharing the cultural backgrounds of little-known peoples is especially important to prevent the loss of more of the world's unique cultures. Translations of cultural artifacts such as *Contes Djerma Nigérien* are increasingly vital.

Folktales highlight important aspects of a people's daily life, and, conversely, knowledge of the culture and history helps readers understand these stories. Little besides millet grows in the Sahel region of Africa where the Zarma make their home, and the crop makes frequent appearances in their folklore. Most Zarma live in villages that are divided into walled off areas, or compounds. Each compound has several huts where a *windi* (family group) lives. The windi has a head male, and each of his wives has her own hut. Livestock are shared and taken care of by the boys, while the girls help pound millet and take care of younger children. Huts are typically round with mud walls and straw roofs.[6]

Before the Zarma were colonized by the French they had a highly stratified social structure. They were led by a chief, or *koy*, who was supported by nobles, *koy-ize*, who held political power. This class was closed and, to consolidate and maintain family wealth, only marriage within the koy-ize class was allowed. The wars of the nineteenth century introduced a new class of warrior. The caste of free men, or *borcin*, who took up arms became *wangari* warriors. Wangari were able to acquire power and prestige, and could own livestock and slaves and collect tribute. Alongside the borcin class was a class called *dumi kayna*, who performed specialized trades, including leather work, weaving, and storytelling. The lowest class, the *banya*, was divided into two categories. The *horso* were captives who had belonged to the same family for several generations and had become trusted servants. The *tam* were trade slaves, sold and given away at will. The status of these slaves was determined by the rank of their masters. Though this structure no longer exists today, the status inherited from earlier times is still used to determine marriages and other agreements.[7]

Zarma lifestyle is heavily influenced by the environment. There are two seasons, the dry season and the rainy season. The fields are plowed and seeded just before the rainy season, and then the millet grows. During the dry season, men are often forced to go "on exodus" to the coasts to find work (as mentioned in "The Hyena and the Hare," this collection's first story). The women stay behind with the children. They eat what has been stored from the harvest, pounding millet and peanuts to make porridge, drinks, and other staple foods.

While the majority of Zarma continue to live in traditional villages, some live in cities like Niamey. They lead modern lives of watching television, going to school, and attending social events. The older generation worries that the youth are losing their connection to their past and are giving up their spiritual lives. The tradition of storytelling in the evenings has been lost, and while younger persons might know the stories, they are, as in North America, merely simple tales learned in childhood.[8]

There are no creation myths in Zarma, and historical records are incomplete prior to the beginning of the twentieth century. More is known about their linguistic cousins, the Songhay. Most Zarma believe they are from the Lake Debo area in Mali, in the far west reaches of the Songhay Empire. Due to this proximity, the two groups share linguistic, religious, and political similarities, and are often simply referred to as the Songhay-Zarma. Today, twice as many Zarma as Songhay live in Niger.

The Songhay originated in what is now Benin, and came to hold power in that region in the tenth and eleventh centuries. The Songhay then moved north to Gao to take advantage of the trans-Saharan trade route that passed through the city, as well as the abundance of gold and salt found in the area. As the Songhay grew rich, the Mali Empire grew jealous and annexed Gao in 1325. The city was reclaimed by the Songhay prince, Sonni Ali Ber, who declared independence and ruled from 1464 to 1492 as the first great king of the Songhay Empire. Following his death, his son briefly held the throne before being overthrown by Askia Mohammed Toure. The Sonni dynasty had been animist and struggled against the Muslims, but Askia Mohammed Toure was a devout Muslim. He led the empire into an era of scholarship and expansion. However, his followers squandered the empire's resources, weakening it. The Moroccans invaded in 1591, and though only one-sixth of their force survived to face the Songhay army, they were armed with superior weapons and were victorious. The surviving Songhay moved to Dendi, near Niamey.

Meanwhile, the Zarma of the Lake Debo area, after repeated attacks from other ethnic groups, began to move toward Gao in the fifteenth century. They adopted a version the Songhay language and continued to migrate south, displacing or assimilating other ethnic groups as they went. The area they settled in became known as Zarmagande. However, due to strife between the leaders, troubles with other ethnic groups, and religious tensions between animists and Muslims, a number of chiefdoms emerged rather than a single, united group.

In 1896, following the division of Africa during the Berlin Conference of 1884–1885, the official borders of Niger were determined and France began its conquest. The French were met with much resistance, especially from the Tuareg who believed the land was rightfully theirs. The French were able to gain a strong foothold in Niger when, in 1898, the chief of Dosso, Zarmakoy Attikou, called on the French military stationed in nearby Benin for help against attacks from neighboring groups.

The French began to impose taxes, which they accepted in kind until 1904, when they brought money to Niger. They did not bring enough currency, however, and because things had to be sold at a much lower price than they were worth, the pauperization of the country began. The French also demanded any supplies they needed to maintain their presence, and forced the people of Niger to build roads or join the military. With fewer men working in the fields, the crops began to rot and food became scarce. These events began the cycle of drought and famine that continues today.[9]

A number of uprisings slowed France's conquest of Niger, namely the Tuareg rebellion of 1916–1917. The British came to France's aid, crushing the Tuareg, and complete pacification of Niger was achieved in 1922, when the country became a colony of France. Niger was run from France through a governor general stationed in Dakar. The country was of little interest to the Western colonial powers because of its lack of natural resources. Native Nigeriens were granted French citizenship following the decentralization of power after World War II, but still had limited political influence.

In the 1950s, two political groups arose in Niger. One, lead by Djibo Bakary, was socialist while the second, led by Hamani Diori, was more conservative. In 1958, Diori's party won the Territorial Assembly elections, and subsequently banned Bakary's party. In September 1958, the National Territory Assembly voted for Niger to become an autonomous state within the French community, and renamed itself the Republic of Niger. In 1960, Niger declared independence.

Independence has not brought peace to Niger. Tuareg revolts occur periodically (the most recent ended in 2008), and have devastating effects on the country. Internal problems with the government abound since the structure is continuously reconfigured due to military coups or civilian outcries against undemocratic practices. For example, between 1989 and 1991 there was only one political party, the National Movement for the Development of Society. At the end of 1990, a general two-day strike was held, forcing the president to allow the nation's first multi-party voting. The next several years were marked by numerous student and civil strikes. An election in 1995 led to a coalition government, which ended up being paralyzed by disagreement between the coalition members. The democratic government was overthrown by army chief Ibrahim Bare Maïnassara, who was then elected president. He was assassinated in 1999.[10] Since then, to prevent one party from holding too much power, Niger's government has been steadily decentralized and the government is semi-presidential, with a president guiding the state and a prime minister heading the government.[11] However, political and economic stability remain unlikely because ethnic differences continue to cause strife, and the country lacks the natural resources needed to lift the populace from its current state of poverty.

While political environments shift and change, the folklore of Niger remains a constant, capturing the life experiences of those who tell it and encompassing the values and morals of the people. There are a variety of story types, each serving a different purpose. *Zarma Folktales of Niger* includes several different kinds of these stories.

Some tales are meant to teach the listeners. Elders use dilemma tales, such as "Betrayal," to teach moral and ethical lessons, and develop argumentation skills.[12] Trickster tales, like "The Two Bandits" and "The Marabout," in which a clever character tries to take advantage of others, reveal how weaknesses can lead to downfall. Other tales reveal the unfairness of life, such as when the hare gets away with his cruelty to the hyena in "The Hyena and the Hare."

A type of tale well known to Western audiences is the "how an animal got a trait" story. "The Election of the Animal King" is one of these, but it also contains instruction about creating a congruous society. It demonstrates applied democracy, as well as the respect paid those who die honorably for their beliefs. "The Three Travelers" similarly illustrates proper behavior by showing the ridiculous reaction of visitors who did not trust their hosts.

The influence of Islam is clear in these stories, not only in the use of common Islamic greetings (*salaam aleikum* or *wa'aleikum as-salaam*), but also in the faith shown in God, as when the stork in "The Election of the Bird King" says: "I can climb into the sky and implore God and know that when I return, I will bring good." Important religious directives, such as being good to those less fortunate and respecting others, are common. For example, the father in "The Three Heroes" says: "You must also respect those who are handicapped because you are not better than them." Morality tales, such as "Sana," focus on similar themes of how to treat others. "The Famine" is both a morality tale and a lesson in how to properly maintain a family. "Sanda Wayzayzé" carries two lessons: work hard, and do not touch what does not belong to you. "The Donkey and the Lion" proves that help can come from unexpected places.

Marriage is one of the most important events in the life of individuals as well as the community in West African culture. While courtship tales differ greatly from those found in Western culture, men in Zarma folktales are found proving themselves to both a woman and her family. "The Farting Girl" seems good only for amusement, but it also illustrates how a man would try to impress himself to a woman—in this case, the dominance of the man is also established, as he succeeds in beating the woman at her own game.

"The Fart Experts" is another funny story that, when further examined, and considering the politics of the area and rivalry between ethnic groups, has an ulterior purpose to show the superiority of the Zarma over the Hausa in both skill and intelligence.

In the end, these stories all reflect a deep sense of humor and a keen interest in justice. There is a great deal to be learned about a people through their folklore, and I hope you will enjoy this glimpse of a little-known culture of the world.

—A.C., October 2009

NOTES

1. Rabah Seffal, *Cultures of the World: Niger.* (New York: Times Publishing Group: 2000), 96.

2. Anne Heinrichs, *Enchantment of the World: Niger.* (New York: Children's Press: 2001), 106.

3. Even though I studied both Hausa and Zarma languages while in Africa, I felt more comfortable in my knowledge of French. Therefore, I translated this collection from that language. Rather than mistranslate some passages in a few of the stories that remained in Hausa or Zarma in the French version, I left them as is in this translation.

4. Central Intelligence Agency World Factbook, "Niger." https://www.cia.gov/library/publications/the-world-factbook/geos/ng.html.

5. Seffal, 48.

6. Heinrichs, 113–114.

7. Deborah Taylor. Lecture, February 11, 2005, Centre de Formation des Cadres d'Alphabétisation, Niamey, Niger.

8. Heinrichs, 111.

9. Deborah Taylor. Lecture, March 16, 2005, Centre de Formation des Cadres d'Alphabétisation, Niamey, Niger.

10. Seffal, 34.

11. Heinrichs, 54–55.

12. William Bascom, "African Dilemma Tales: An Introduction," in *African Folklore*, Richard M. Dorson, ed. (Anchor Books, 1972), 143.

The Hyena and the Hare

ONE DAY, ALL the wild animals decided to plant a field of millet. They cleared the land, plowed it, and seeded it when the first rains fell. They plowed and weeded it at just the right time to produce a good harvest and filled a large granary with the millet. Then, a meeting was convened.

"We've harvested all we can before going on exodus," said one animal to the rest. "At the first rain of next year, we'll all return home and divide up our harvest."

So it was said, so it was done.

After everyone had left, the hare moved in next to the granary with his family. From time to time, he

<1>

took some heads of millet and gave them to his wives, who pounded them. Every time he took some, the hare searched for hyena dung to fill in the space. He continued his thefts until all the millet had been eaten.

The first rain fell, and all the animals returned home. The clever hare did not appear immediately. Once everyone else had arrived, he told his wife to pour water over his whole body. Then he ran to join his friends.

"Oh! Brother, you have traveled much," they exclaimed. "Where were you?"

"I was in Haway, Safay, and Sasabay, on the way to Bargay, Hinay, and Dwayay."

"You really have been all over. No wonder you're sweating so much."

"Open the granary!"

To everyone's great surprise, there was only one head of millet left. The granary was full of hyena excrement. They all turned and looked at the hyena in astonishment.

"The hyena gobbled up all the millet."

<2>

"It wasn't me, I swear."

They searched for a way to determine the thief. "At nightfall, we'll lie side by side and the moonlight will fall on the guilty one."

"Yes, yes!" all the animals agreed.

When they lay down for the night, the hare lay next to the hyena and said, "You're not the one who stole the millet, big brother. They just want to blame you."

"God is great," the hyena replied.

Everyone slept, except for the guilty hare. An hour into the night, the moonlight fell on his chest. He moved it onto the chest of the hyena and woke the others.

"Wake up, wake up! The moon has fallen on the chest of big brother hyena."

Barely awake, the other animals began to hit the hyena until he could no longer move.

The hare approached him and said, "Brother, they will kill you, but you're not the one who ate the millet."

"Little brother," replied the hyena in a melancholy voice, "I'm not yet dead."

<3>

At these words, the hare called the others back, telling them the hyena was still alive. They gathered and beat him again.

"Now my big brother is dead."

"No, I'm still not dead. I won't die until my head is broken."

The hare called again to the others to come and crack open the hyena's head. Just as he had said would happen, the hyena died.

<4>

The Donkey and the Lion

DURING A YEAR of drought, a donkey and his wife decided to go on exodus. They walked for a whole day. At nightfall, they noticed a house in the middle of the forest and presented themselves there.

"*Salaam aleikum*," said the donkey.

"*Wa'aleikum as-salaam*," replied the owner of the house.

To their great surprise, the donkey couple saw a lion before them. They were frightened, but quickly regained their composure.

"Who are you?" demanded the lion.

"I am *maï-biddiga* (a gun carrier). I am a hunter because of my strong ears."

<5>

"Perfect. That's lucky. But aren't you donkeys?"

"No, no. This is just a disguise."

With that, the lion gave them a bed for the night. The donkey's wife, gripped by fear, said to her husband, "We must run away from here, or the lion will eat us."

"Oh, don't worry. He'll let us leave."

Early the next morning, the lion woke his guest so they could go hunting. The two men left, but since the donkey didn't know how to hunt, only the lion caught game. They returned home. The same thing happened on all their trips.

One day, after the lion and the donkey had left, the lioness invited the donkey's wife into her room and offered to remove the lice from her head. The donkey accepted and gave her head to the lioness, who took advantage of the opportunity to confirm that the donkey's ears were not rifles.

When the men returned from the hunt, the lioness told her husband that their guests really were donkeys, but the lion did not believe her. To find out for certain, he pretended to be ill and told his wife to

<6>

fetch the donkey. The donkey ran in to find the lion suffering and asked him what was wrong.

"Today, my entire body hurts, so you must go and find us something to eat."

"No problem," said the donkey, who realized the lions' plan. "Is there a pond nearby?" he asked the lioness.

"Yes. The elephant and the other animals go there to drink water."

"Good," replied the donkey.

He went to the pond, hid himself in a bush, and waited. A moment later, the elephant appeared, followed by the other animals who had to wait until the pachyderm was finished drinking to have their turn.

The elephant finished. The animals had just begun to drink when the donkey burst out of the bush shouting: "Wohi-wohi-tico-tico." Terrified, the animals scattered. There were blows from paws, blows from horns, blows from mouths, and the big ones crushed the small ones. It was worse than a battlefield. Satisfied, the donkey returned to the lion's

<7>

house and asked the women to collect the animals he had killed. They left to get them.

Surprised, the lion said to his wife, "See, he is a maï-biddiga. We even heard the sound of his gun."

"That's true. You're right, dear."

They ate well, and afterward the donkey announced his intention to continue his journey. The lion asked for one of his guns.

"Oh no! I am the only one able to care for them."

The donkey couple left and the lions accompanied them to the edge of the forest where they said good-bye.

A passing hyena caught the scent of the donkeys and set out to pursue them. On his way, he met the returning lion and asked him, "Did you see any donkeys come by this way?"

"No, they're not donkeys. It's a maï-biddiga and his wife."

"Those donkeys tricked you. Let's go catch them."

They returned to pursue the donkeys together, but the lion hung back. When the donkey's wife looked behind her, she saw the hyena following

<8>

them and said to her husband, "Dear, the hyena is behind us."

"Tie up my front legs and you'll see. At a time like this a donkey's back legs serve him well as a weapon."

The hyena had closed in on the donkey and was ready to attack when he received a great kick of the legs. He fell and lost consciousness. The donkey turned to the watching lion and told him to take the meat. The lion leapt at the hyena, who cried out that he was not dead, but the lion continued and took the body home, thanking the maï-biddiga who was able to kill animals so well with his hooves.

So, the donkey was saved from the lion and continued on his journey with his wife.

<9>

The Three Travelers

THREE TRAVELERS CAME to a village at night. They presented themselves at the first house.

"How are you?"

"Good, my friends. Where are you coming from at this hour of the night?"

"We left on a trip, and now it's night. We would like to stay here."

"No problem. You are welcome."

They were offered food and drink before being taken to the hut where they would sleep. They lay down, and in the middle of the night, one of the three turned over, put his hand on a squash and gave a start. He woke the man next to him and asked him

<11>

if his head was on his neck. The man responded yes, so the first man asked the third, who also responded affirmatively. The two who had been asked wanted to know why he was wondering. The first man replied that he had a head in his hand. Suddenly frightened, the three men searched for the exit. They destroyed the entire hut in their terror. Hearing the commotion, the head of the family rose and went to the hut.

"What's going on?"

"There's a head in the hut."

"Oh! Those are the squashes I picked this morning."

<12>

The Fart Experts

THERE WERE ONCE two men, one Hausa and one Zarma, who said they were fart experts. When they heard about each other, they decided to fatten bulls for a farting contest. Whoever won would keep the bulls. The Hausa man went to the house of the Zarma fart expert. When he arrived, he found no one but a five-day-old baby. Scarcely had the man entered the compound, than he began to fart.

bout "*Salaam aleikum.*"

The baby responded immediately like this: *bout* "My father has gone to the fields." *bout* "My mother has gone to find bark to make me an infusion of tea."

<13>

Astonished, the Hausa expert approached the house and looked inside. He did not see anyone. He heard the newborn: *bout* "My father has gone to the fields." *bout* "My mother has gone to find bark to make me an infusion of tea."

The young man explored the house. He saw the tiny feet rising from a *pagne* and realized it was a newborn. Afraid, he said, "A newborn is making this noise, and if the father finds me here, he will kill me and take my bull."

After he left, the mother returned and the newborn told her the story. Angry, the mother said, "You are worthless." *bouout* "You could have farted and taken the bull. You are not like your father." *bouout* "You are not like your mother."

At that moment, the Zarma fart expert came home and the newborn told him: *bout* "Father," *bout* "a man with a bull" *bout* "has come here with a bull for a farting contest."

The father responded, *bouout* "Where is he?" *bouout*

"He followed that path."

<14>

bouout "I will go find him. I must bring the bull back here."

He bent over and farted in the direction of his opponent. It caught up with the Hausa expert, killed him, and brought back the Zarma expert's bull.

<15>

Sanda Wayzayzé

ONCE UPON A time, there was a man named Sanda Wayzayzé. Before the first rains fell, he thoroughly prepared his field. When it rained, Sanda planted. People began plowing. Sanda plowed his field once and then again a second time. Then he said that, now that the work was done, he would travel.

Sanda returned to his field. He scratched his head and found a louse. He took it and pulled on its ear until it cried "ciit."

Sanda said, "Don't bother with 'ciit'. I swear to God that if I return from my trip and find that a single leaf of a head of millet is gone from my field, I will burn you and pour your ashes into the river."

<17>

He put the louse on the leaf of a head of millet and left.

The winter months passed nicely and everything the people had planted grew. They went into the fields and harvested some ears, which they roasted and ate.

"We should go look at the field," Sanda's second wife said to the first. "We haven't visited it since Sanda left. We know nothing about it. We don't even know whether or not the birds have picked it clean."

"You're right," replied the first wife. "We'll go tomorrow morning."

The next day they went to the field and were surprised to find that the millet and the cowpeas were fine. In fact, not one field in the whole town was doing as well as their husband's.

They decided to take some heads of millet to grill for the children and some cowpeas for themselves. One of the wives bent next to a stalk of millet. She was about to cut the head when the louse cried, "Who is in Sanda's field? Sanda Wayzayzé plowed his field step by step, and plowed it a second time.

Sanda has gone to fight in Katsina, Timbuktu, Yaayiré, and Zanzaw. No one may touch Sanda's field!"

The women ran away as fast as their legs could carry them. Before they had even left the field, they shat in their pagnes. They wanted to pass by the village, but some people stopped them and asked them what was wrong. They replied that something had frightened them in their husband's field, and they had no idea if it was something in the air or on the ground. The fathers-in-law of Sanda decided to go the next day to see what was wrong in their son-in-law's field. They left the house in the late morning carrying arrows. They checked the entire field, but found absolutely nothing. They noticed that there was no other field like it in the village.

One of the two wanted to take a head of millet, and the louse cried, "Who is in Sanda's field? Sanda Wayzayzé plowed his field step by step, and plowed it a second time. Sanda has gone to fight in Katsina, Timbuktu, Yaayiré, and Zanzaw. No one may touch Sanda's field!"

<19>

The two old men ran away. Before they got to the village, their pants were dirtied; they had shat in them. A man noticed them, gave a cry, and invited the people to come look at the fathers-in-law of Sanda.

"They've come back from the field of their son-in-law, frightened. Come, we want to know what you saw."

The two old men recounted what had happened, but nobody would believe it. They all decided to visit the field the next day. Early the next morning, men on horseback and men armed with knives set out. They checked the entire field, but found nothing. Sanda's cousin said he wouldn't leave the field until he had collected some millet. He was about to take a head when suddenly the louse cried, "Who is in Sanda's field? Sanda Wayzayzé plowed his field step by step, and plowed it a second time. Sanda has gone to fight in Katsina, Timbuktu, Yaayiré, and Zanzaw. No one may touch Sanda's field!"

At these words, the men began to cry "Waaa, waaa-waaa!" and ran away. The strong trampled the weak;

<20>

others shat in their pants. They ran past the village where the women and children remained. The women went in search of their husbands. Just then, Sanda returned from his journey. His fathers-in-law went to welcome him back.

"Sanda, we have something to tell you."

The father of the first wife started, "Sanda, your field is dangerous. I advise you to go and harvest the millet with your brother-in law since he has two granaries' worth every year."

The second father-in-law repeated the same thing.

Sanda demanded to know why he couldn't go to his field. "I want to go there. I fought in the war. What else could I possibly fear?"

The next day, he told his wives to get ready to go to the field. The women told him they would not budge from the house. The husband insisted and his wives followed. They walked slowly behind him. When they arrived at the field, Sanda ordered his wives to take an ear. The wives refused because they knew what would happen. They told him to go ahead himself. Sanda relieved his guard, the louse

<21>

who had been in his hair, and began to harvest. He thanked the louse.

That evening, the wives of Sanda returned to the village, the heads of millet and the beans on their head. Angry, the villagers wanted to know why Sanda could take his millet without anything happening. They thought he must be a magician.

Sanda arrived and showed them the louse. "This is what upset you so. Truly."

The villagers hid their shame.

<22>

Betrayal

A HUNTER WHO lived in the forest with his family ate only meat. One day, he went out to find game, but returned empty-handed. For three days, he found nothing. He decided to go down to the river. There, he noticed a starving alligator who was unable to get to the water because he had walked too far away from the river. The man was about to kill him when the alligator called to him and said, "I haven't eaten in days. If you carry me to the river, no alligator will ever eat you or a member of your family."

The man thought about it and accepted the proposition. He carried the alligator to the edge of the river. Before he could put him down, the animal

<23>

asked to be taken to the middle of the river. The man took the alligator to the middle of the river and put him down. But, when the man tried to leave the water, the alligator took him by the hand and said, "I won't let you go. I'm hungry. I want to eat you."

At the same moment, the man noticed a horse coming to drink. He called and explained his situation, but the horse said to him, "I can't help you because I have been betrayed by a man. After I gave him twelve foals, he ignored me. I managed to eat something, and then escaped."

After that, the man saw a cow and a donkey, both of whom also refused to help him. They all said they had been betrayed by man.

The alligator was about to kill the man when a hare appeared. "What's going on?" asked the hare.

The man told him the story. The clever hare told the alligator and the man that they should get out of the water so he could decide who was right. The naïve alligator got out of the water and carried them a kilometer from the river. There, the hare asked the hunter to demonstrate how he had carried the alligator to the river.

<24>

The man took the alligator, tied him up, and set him on his head.

"Good," said the hare. "Now, take us to your home. Your family will eat today."

The alligator struggled, but was taken by the hunter and killed. The hare remained in the bushes. Upon entering the village, the man met some children who were going hunting. "Go quickly!" he told them. "A giant hare is in the bushes nearby. You can make a great feast."

The children left and found the hare. Hounded by the children and their dogs, the hare was saved by a heron who took him in his beak and carried him to the shore. The hare, acknowledging the heron, said, "Years ago, I was told I would do charity for a white thing. I turned a deaf ear, and so failed at life. Now that I've seen you, I know how I'll accomplish my good deed."

The hare killed the heron that had saved him and distributed the meat.

So we must ask: was it the alligator, the hunter, or the hare who betrayed the other?

<25>

The Marabout

THERE WAS ONCE a marabout who wanted to visit Mecca. He decided to go there on horseback. On the way, he came across a pond. "I must rest here for the day," he said. Just then a hyena came to drink.

"*Salaam aleikum*," the hyena said.

"*Wa'aleikum as-salaam*," the marabout responded.

"How has your day been?"

"Good."

"Where are you going, sir?" the hyena asked.

"I am going to Mecca," said the marabout.

"Ah, Mecca. How many days have you been on the road?"

<27>

"A long time, my friend. I've been traveling for two months."

"It's not worth it," said the hyena. "Your horse is weary. Two months is a long time. The other day, I took a marabout to Mecca in just fifteen days."

"Could you take me?" the marabout asked.

"I will take you, as long as you let me eat your horse," the hyena replied. "There is no one here to whom you can entrust it anyway."

So, the marabout gave him his horse. The hyena gobbled it up and said to the marabout, "You must take care of yourself. I can't serve as your horse. You can rest over there if you want." Then he left. The astonished marabout rested, uncertain what to do. A little while later, a hare came to drink from the pond. He noticed the marabout holding his head in his hands.

"Dear marabout," the hare said. "Why are you in such a state?"

"Funny you should ask, hare. I left for Mecca on my horse and someone came and found me by the side of this pond and asked me where I was going.

<28>

I told him I was on my way to Mecca and that I had been traveling for two months. He replied that my horse was weary and that he could take me there in fifteen days as long as I let him eat my horse. He devoured it and left me here."

"You will have your horse" said the hare. "I will get it for you right away. Where is the horse's saddle?"

"It's over there," replied the marabout.

The hare took it and went in search of the hyena. He came to edge of a hole and began to whimper. "My sister is married. We slaughtered a bull but there is no one to cut it up." With one jump the hyena leapt out to meet the hare.

"What's wrong?" he asked.

"We slaughtered a bull to celebrate my sister's marriage, but there is no one to skin it."

"Is that why you're crying? Don't cry. Your father has decided that I am your guardian. It was necessary for you to come ask for me. So good, let's go. Climb on my back. Then we'll go more quickly."

Beforehand, the hare had hidden the marabout's riding supplies. When they reached the spot where the

<29>

rope was hidden, the hare said, "My fingers hurt, wait a moment and I'll get a rope to protect my hands."

The hyena agreed, and then they continued on.

When they arrived at place where the saddle was hidden, the hare began to move around a lot and said, "My bottom is hurting, if you let me use this saddle, it would relieve me."

"Take it!"

They continued on their way. So it was that the hare retrieved all of the marabout's riding equipment, one piece at a time, before arriving at the pond where the man waited.

When they arrived at the pond, the hyena said to the hare, "My in-laws live this way. I broke one of their ladles and don't want to run into them."

"Then we won't go there," replied the hare. He pretended to obey, but led the hyena to the marabout. "Look, here is your horse," the hare said to the marabout.

The hyena began to tremble.

"Thank you very much, dear hare. The Lord will repay you."

<30>

The marabout mounted the hyena and got on his way. "You told me you took someone to Mecca in fifteen days," he said. "Therefore, I would also like to make it in fifteen days."

The marabout made the hyena run until the animal's whole body was covered in blood. They arrived at a village where they decided to pass the night. The marabout asked the people not to separate him from his horse. They brought the hyena grass, which he would not eat. A skin was brought on which the marabout could pray. The hyena threw itself on the skin and took a bite. At sunrise, they returned to the road to Mecca. They arrived on the evening of the Pilgrimage.

In the morning, the marabout said to the innkeeper: "You must not let your children approach my horse. He is untamed. Do not take him anything to eat or drink either."

The head of the family said, "I understand. Anyone who turns a deaf ear will be punished."

The children got together and talked about climbing on the hyena, each in turn. "I'll take the horse of my father's guest to drink," said a boy.

<31>

His friends replied, "We were told not to go near it. Heed the warning!"

"That's because he doesn't want us riding it," the child said. "The guest who came the day before yesterday had a tame horse that I rode."

Even before he reached the door, the hyena tore into the child's thigh. The people began shouting, "Come, come, the horse of the guest at the inn has torn a child's thigh."

They chased the hyena, and he ran. He ran until he could no longer hear the echoes of his pursuers. He stopped, rested, and then continued on his way. Soon, he met a passerby.

"Come here!" he said.

The man approached.

"Go find wood to grill yourself," the hyena told him. "I would like to eat your meat, and have your fat to soothe the injuries the villagers gave me."

The man began to cry as he collected the wood. Luckily, he ran into the hare. The hare asked him if he had met the hyena. "He told me to get wood so he could grill me because he needs my meat and my fat."

<32>

"You must do your work slowly. Then he'll ask what is happening. I will say: '*A bi biya zaaci.*' And you will respond: '*A gaskiyaa ne.*' Then he'll ask who's there, and you will say it's a marabout in search of his horse. Then he'll run to save himself."

The man continued to collect wood.

"Why are you going so slow?" the hyena cried.

"I'm coming!"

"*A bi biya zaaci,*" said the hare.

The man responded with "*A gaskiyaa ne,*" and the hyena, who did not speak Hausa, asked who was there.

"It's someone looking for his horse."

"Don't answer. Wait until I get away." The hyena ran and disappeared.

<33>

The Election of the Bird King

ONE DAY, THE birds decided to elect a king from among themselves. For this purpose, a meeting was called. The candidates were Zébane the vulture, Kaoua the eagle, a hawk, and Bourtou the pelican. A sasabri, smallest of the birds, wanted to run as well, but his candidacy was not approved because the judge deemed him too small to be their king.

Unhappy, the sasabri returned from the meeting and told the other sasabris of the judge's decision. Disappointed, the sasabris convened and decided to band together from then on so they could face down attacks from other birds. Since that day, sasabris have always lived in groups.

<35>

Zébane and Kaoua were the strongest, and the birds voted unanimously that one of them should be their king.

"Why us?" Kaoua asked.

"Kaoua! You can fly up to the second of the seven heavens," the audience replied. "And Zébane, you can fly up to the fourth heaven."

Because of this reasoning, Kaoua withdrew in favor of Zébane and offered to be his assistant.

One day, the king asked each bird which post he would like to fill to constitute the court.

"I am a farmer," Bourtou said. "I prefer to help the people of the court."

"I am the shepherd," said the heron. "I will watch over all the animals the king buys or receives as gifts."

"I am the messenger," said the raven. "I charge myself with bringing and taking messages."

"I am in charge of all the court's meat," said the carrion bird.

"I am ready to transport a hundred puppets for the feasts when you want them," said the falcon.

<36>

"I am the bard," said Kagou. "When one hears my song, '*Koumaré-Kouma, Koumaré-Kouma,*' one knows the king is near."

"I guard the court with my eyes," said the owl, "for when I look at someone, he understands me. Besides which, I consult the earth and foresee the future."

"I am the police officer," said the hawk. "With my claws I can carry anyone to court who refuses to comply with a summoning."

Thus the court was established. The king asked the hawk what he would do to punish the sasabris for abandoning the court. The hawk responded, "Majesty, I think you must have fifty sasabris at every meal (morning, noon, and night)." And the king ordered the hawk to bring him his first fifty.

In the meantime, the sasabris agreed on a strategy for attacking any bird that came to do them harm. They came up with a password: "Tchir-Tchar." Upon hearing that word, all the sasabris would attack at once.

The hawk left to find the sasabris and told them the purpose of his mission. All of a sudden, one of them

<37>

cried, "Tchir-Tchar," and they all began attacking the hawk with their beaks and talons until the hawk could not even raise his head. Unable to hold out, the hawk took refuge in a bush where he died of hunger and thirst while a guard of sasabris circled his refuge.

Victorious, the sasabris regrouped for the next attack.

The stork, a migrating bird, arrived at the king's court and was asked his role. "I am a marabout," the stork replied. "I can climb into the sky and implore God and know that when I return, I will bring good. That is why storks only come at the approach of the rainy season."

The king accepted this.

When it became clear that the hawk was not coming back, the king sent the falcon to see what had happened. The falcon left, and asked the sasabris if they had seen the hawk. The order was given, "Tchir-Tchar," and the falcon suffered the same fate as the hawk.

Anxious, the king asked the owl to consult the earth to find out what was going on.

<38>

That done, the owl said: "Majesty, the sasabris are stronger than us. They agreed to unite their forces. They mounted a plan of attack and killed the hawk and falcon by beating them with their claws and beaks."

Having heard the news, the king sent the carrion bird, whom he believed was strong, but the carrion bird suffered the same fate as the others. When he did not return, the king proposed that the other birds go. They all refused because they were weaker than those who had already gone. Soudé, another bird in the king's court, proposed that the king send his assistant. But the king sent a crow, who also suffered the same fate.

The king called the owl to consult the earth a second time. The owl repeated the same news as before. Furious, the king decided to go himself and the owl said to him, "Majesty, you risk death by passing the fourth heaven that you know and going up to the seventh."

As king, Zébane could not back away from danger. He climbed up to the fourth heaven to better see the

<39>

sasabris and decided to descend upon them. But they were cleverer than him, and scattered. The king dove toward the earth, but could not prevail and climbed into the sky again. He was chased by the sasabris into the seventh heaven, where he took refuge and stayed for a hundred years. The sasabris, who could not pass the sixth heaven, descended and became kings of the birds. Since that day all the birds have been afraid of the sasabris.

<40>

The Election of the Animal King

ONE DAY, ALL the wild animals decided to elect a king from among themselves. The elephant, the lion, the tiger, and the buffalo were the candidates. The elephant, who directed the meeting, gave the choice to the other animals.

The animals retired to deliberate. Some proposed to elect the lion, but others were against this because the lion is impatient and might kill them if he got angry. Others preferred the buffalo, but the same remarks were made regarding him.

"As for the tiger, he is very cagey. Let's choose the elephant because he is big and very patient." Thus, the elephant was unanimously elected king of the

<41>

animals. He took the floor to thank them and asked them to set up court.

The lion chose to be a soldier. The tiger asked to be a police officer. Kabi, a fast runner, proposed that he be the king's courier. The hyena wanted to be the guard, but was opposed by the rhinoceros, and there proceeded a contest of force between the two. The hyena bit his adversary three times in a row, but the rhinoceros felt nothing. As for the rhinoceros, he delivered a single blow to the hyena who, deprived of a paw, turned tail. Thus the court was established that day, and the animals lived together.

One day, some hunters traveled through the entire bush and found nothing. Tired, they decided to go to the shore of a pond and see if they would have any luck there. When they arrived at the pond, they climbed a big tree and surveyed the area.

After a while, the king sent the buffalo to collect water. The starving hunters shot at him with poisoned arrows. The buffalo ran and hid behind a bush, but could not escape the intrepid hunters. He

<42>

was killed and, after they had eaten all they could, his meat was hung in the tree.

The king, who had noticed that the buffalo did not return, sent Kabi to see what was wrong. He left and saw the buffalo's meat hanging from the tree. The hunters saw him, and sent their dogs to pursue him, but he escaped and told the king what he had found.

"*Wallahi!*" cried the king. "The buffalo himself— now who can bring me water?"

The lion volunteered. "If I don't return, you'll know that something bad has happened," he said. "But I think I will return."

The lion left for the pond and began to roar. A hunter aimed well and hit him in the neck. Furious, the lion knocked down the trees around him. He managed to break a branch of the tree the hunters were in. A second arrow whistled. The lion jumped, but accidentally fell on his neck and died. He suffered the same fate as the buffalo, and his skin was hung from the tree as well.

The animal king asked Kabi to go look again. Upon his return, he reported the same findings. The

<43>

king grew anxious and asked for another volunteer. The tiger went and suffered the same fate as his predecessors. Now, there was no one left but the king, the rhinoceros, and the smaller animals. The rhinoceros proposed to the king that he himself should go because that would show the smaller animals that the elephant was an able king.

The elephant, upon leaving, began to uproot all the trees as he went. He arrived at the pond, lifted his head and his trunk to trumpet, and was struck by an arrow between his nose and his trunk. Furious, he prepared to attack. A second arrow struck him behind the ear, and a third in his flank. Poisoned by the arrows, the king fell and died.

Now the hunters had all the meat. No one saw the king return, and the rhinoceros said to the others that he would go, but first he would prepare a concoction against the iron and the poison. On the eve of his departure, he asked the large tortoise to play the *kora* (a traditional guitar). The tortoise sang a eulogy: "Whether the hunters like it or not, the rhinoceros will drink from the pond." The rhinoceros was very flattered.

<44>

The rhinoceros went to the pond. Under the watch of the hunters, he bathed in the mud. Gripped by fear, one of the hunters asked the others to leave the animal alone, but they refused and began to shoot. An arrow struck him and broke. So it went until all the hunters' arrows were gone. Furious, the rhinoceros threw himself in the mud once more. The hunters, out of arrows, wanted to flee, but the rhinoceros attacked them. He killed one, but the others succeeded in disappearing mysteriously. They related the facts to an old hunter magician, who gave them a concoction and one well-poisoned arrow and said to them, "Go and kill the rhinoceros, but one of you will be hurt."

The hunters returned and attacked again. The rhinoceros, who could take no more, returned to the animals. He called to the giant tortoise and said, "I will die, but before that, I will kill a man. I want you to play my eulogy."

The unhappy tortoise swore that after the death of the rhinoceros he would never play his guitar again. The rhinoceros returned to the pond and as he had

<45>

foreseen, killed one of the hunters and then died from the poison in the magician's arrow. Upon the death of the rhinoceros, the tortoise broke his guitar and reversed the calabash on his back. That is why the tortoise has a shell.

<46>

The Famine

THERE WAS A big drought—not a drop of rain for a year. In the village, no one had food. Only a few trees grew. One family had only cooked leaves to eat. Each morning, the wife and her children went in search of more leaves. It went like this until one day the rain fell. The men took advantage by sowing seeds, plowing, and weeding. One morning, the men headed to their fields, and the head of the family stopped on the shore of a pond that he found in his field. "I didn't know there was a pond in my field." A bird in a tree repeated what he said word for word. Surprised, the man asked where this bird that repeated everything came from.

<47>

"Where does this Zarma that repeats everything I say come from?" countered the bird.

"I'll throw a stone at you if you repeat what I say again," said the man.

"If you throw one at me, I'll do the same."

"All right." The man took a stone and threw it. The bird took a millet ball and threw it. The man repeated his action, and the bird did the same. The man took the two balls and ate them without mixing them with water, then continued on his way. He spent the whole day plowing and plowing. In the evening, he returned home, stopping by the pond. "Ha!" he said. "I am going to rest."

"Ha! I am going to rest," the bird repeated.

The man said the same thing he had the last time, and the bird again repeated everything. After retrieving the two balls of millet, the man ate a ball and a half, hid the rest, and went home.

When he arrived home, his wife told their children to bring him the cooked leaves.

"Take back your leaves. I don't want them," said the father.

<48>

"Look, children, your father cannot stand the hunger. He'll die, the poor thing."

The man waited until his wife left and then ran to take a calabash and a ladle, which he hid in the sack he would take to the field. Early the next morning, he took it on the road. When he arrived at the pond, he repeated the same phrases as before and the bird repeated them back. The man took the two balls, mixed them with water and continued on his way. Returning in the evening, he stopped at his accustomed place beside the pond, found the balls he had mixed and tossed them down his throat before entering his house. His family presented him with cooked leaves and again he refused them.

One day, the youngest of the family said to his mother, "Mama, I want to know why my father no longer wants to eat what we eat. Tomorrow I will find out."

The next day, at the muezzin's call for the morning prayer, the child got up and hid himself by the road to the field. After the prayer, the father took the road. The boy saw his father from his hiding place and let him

<49>

pass. He followed him slowly. When his father arrived at the shore of the pond, he spoke with the bird and the hiding child heard everything. The boy waited until after his father mixed the rest of the balls in water and drank it and continued on his way and then presented himself to the bird as well.

"Ha! I am going to rest."

"Ha! I am going to rest," repeated the bird.

"Who there is repeating what I say?"

"Who is the little Zarma repeating what I say?"

"Watch out! I'll throw a rock at you."

"If you throw one at me, I'll throw one at you, too."

The child threw a rock; the bird threw a millet ball at him. The child continued to throw rocks until he'd gathered about twenty balls. He made a container using vines and branches and carried them home. Upon seeing him, his mother cried: "My dear youngest has arrived, and he has something on his head. He's carrying something!"

The child placed his package on the ground and all his brothers and sisters gathered. "It's millet balls.

<50>

They're millet balls! We'll treat ourselves." They began to eat the balls. After a while, the father finished his plowing and wanted to go home. He stopped at the pond to collect his balls. He mixed them in water, and calmly headed home. Upon his arrival, they presented him with the cooked leaves.

"I am not a billy goat. Not even a sheep would eat those leaves. Take them away."

"This is three days now that you haven't eaten a thing," his wife replied. "You will die if you don't watch out, *aro ga labduru.*"

"That's not your problem. Leave me alone," he said. "*Aro ga labduru.*"

The next day, the man returned to the field. He stopped by the pond, recited his terms as always, took two balls, mixed them in water, and then continued on his way.

After he left, the youngest son told his mother, brothers, and sisters to take bags and containers to their father's pond. So it was done, and the youngest, who already knew the words, said them. The bird, in return, threw millet balls at them. The family gath-

<51>

ered many pebbles and the boy continued to throw them. Suddenly—"pat"—a stone struck the bird and it fell dead. They hurried and left the place, carrying away the dead bird. When they got back to the village, they took two full bags of millet balls to the chief and recounted the story.

That evening, the father headed home, and stopping at the pond he said, "I am going to rest." He did not hear the bird, so he repeated his words a second time. Nothing. A third time. Nothing. He began to walk around the tree. He saw feathers on the ground and realized that someone else had been there. "They killed my bird. I will call on the village chief. He'll set them right!"

At home, he was presented with a calabash full of millet balls that had been mixed with water. He scolded his family. "You are the ones who killed my bird. Get up and go to the village chief."

"Go yourself," his wife said. "When the chief summons us, we will go."

The man left to see the chief and told him what had happened. The chief sent for the man's family.

<52>

The chief asked the man to repeat what he had said. He recounted the story again.

"Did you bring your family any balls?" asked the village chief.

"No," the man replied.

The chief ordered him to be beaten. He was whipped until he bled. He staggered home. His wife brought him balls in a calabash.

That was truly an irresponsible head of the family.

<53>

The Three Heroes

ONE DAY, A father called to his son and counseled him on life for a long time.

"You must respect everyone and obey the orders of your elders. You must not spend time with bandits and hoodlums. You must understand what I am trying to tell you. These are the most important things for a responsible person to know. I do not know when I will die, and you're old enough now to learn. If you live your life well, God will protect you. You must also respect those who are handicapped because you are not better than them. That is what God wants."

"Father, I understand and will act accordingly."

<55>

In the village, two other fathers gave the same advice to their sons and made sure they understood. The three exemplary boys met where the youths of the village gathered. They chatted and then returned home. After a while, they became friends. They asked their fathers for their own fields to cultivate, and their fathers agreed. Every rainy season, they helped their fathers plow in the family field before doing the same in their own fields. Thus they came to know their own strength. They never undertook anything without informing their relatives first.

In the other corner of the village, there was also an exemplary girl. Since the age of two, she had always been with her mother, helping with the housekeeping. When she reached the age of seven, her mother called to her and her father and the two of them gave sage advice to their daughter.

"This sage advice was given to me by my mother, and now it is my turn to offer it to you. You must be good to men in order to be loved. You must tell me everything you do, and I will help you. Today, I will teach you to work with cotton."

<56>

The girl began to work with cotton. She made a number of pieces, which her mother collected and gave to the weaver to make pagnes. Every rainy season, the girl helped her mother work in the okra and peanut fields before working at home. Her mother did nothing with the crops except sell them and feed the animals, until the girl became very rich.

One day, the girl told her mother she wanted to visit a relative. Her mother allowed it. On her way, the girl met the three exemplary friends. She stepped off the path to hide behind a tree, wrapped a pagne around her head, and then continued on her way. At first sight, the three boys fell in love with the girl, but none of them showed it. Right away, each returned home and presented the problem to his relatives, and the relatives decided to go to the girl's house to ask for her hand. So the fathers of the three friends met at the house of the same girl for the same reason. The girl's parents listened attentively as each came and spoke with them in turn. They asked if it was the family or the boys themselves who would pay for the marriage since a husband must be responsible; a lazy

<57>

boy who does not respect his wife or his in-laws will never be responsible.

"Our sons are courageous," said the relatives. "They work hard and will raise the money to cover the expenses of their own marriage."

Knowing that the outlook was favorable, the father said to his daughter, "I will not choose. The good Lord will sort it out."

He asked the first father to go and fetch his son to chat with the girl. At home, the father announced the news to his son, accompanied by a griot. They went to the girl's house and were welcomed and shown to the girl by a great aunt. The boy and girl spoke quietly for a long time. The girl wanted a respectable husband, so she decided to test the boy to make sure he wasn't just a skirt chaser. She lay across his legs and teased him. He did not respond, but continued to chat until evening. As he took his leave of the girl, he put some money on the mat. The next day, the second suitor arrived and also chatted quietly; and finally the third. Each time before leaving, they left money on the mat.

<58>

Afterward, the girl's relatives called her and asked her if she had chosen between the three suitors. "Yes, dear relatives, I spoke with all three. They have the same character and left the same amount of money on the mat. It's impossible for me to choose. They are all exemplary. To sort it out, I must determine who is the most courageous." Her relatives agreed because it was up to her to decide.

"How will you decide between them?"

"You know the village next to ours? A famous hairdresser lives there. I would like to go to her for the wedding celebration. The women of our village won't go there for fear of being eaten by the lioness that has lived between the villages for a long time. There are also two genies on the way, one named Naturunku and the other Maykasumba. They attack people. I want to invite the boys to come with me to the hairdresser. Then I'll see who is the most courageous."

The girl sent the griot to tell the boys. The boys told their relatives. The mothers were worried. "Our brave sons will be killed because of this girl," they

<59>

thought. The fathers remained calm and gave their sons permission to go with the girl. Despite all the dangers, she decided to go with them. While the children were growing up, they had never disobeyed anyone, they had respected their elders, and they had never said they were better than someone else; thus the Lord watched over them.

The first griot invited another griot to come and sing praises to the families. They spent the morning in a hut with the girl. At midday, the travelers left the village. They walked and walked. During the journey, the girl spoke to no one. She didn't want the boys to think that she liked one more than another. When they reached the territory of the lioness, the girl said, "First, I am thirsty; second, I am cold; third, I would like one of you to stay with me because I'm afraid the lioness will devour me."

The boys chose who would stay with her, who would search for fire, and who would fetch water. Then they left to complete their tasks. The genie called Naturunku had a pit in which he boiled his victims, and Maykasumba grilled his in a giant fire.

<60>

The girl said to the boy who stayed with her, "We must not make any noise, and we must not cough, otherwise the lioness will find us here."

They sat atop a dead tree trunk. The boy made himself cough, and coughed three times. Before he had finished the third, the lioness sprang out. With one blow, she uprooted the trunk of the dead tree that had been more than a hundred years old. She thought it was the boy. She turned around, saw that the boy lived and pounced at him. The young man lowered himself and brandished his saber, but missed. The lioness pounced at him anew. The young man once more swung his saber, but missed again. A third time, the lioness pounced and the young man's saber slipped from his grasp and fell. He found himself face to face with the lioness about to pounce on him. Suddenly, he lowered himself and tackled the lioness's back paws, throwing her off balance. Then, taking the trunk of the tree that had fallen, he knocked her back. The animal flew through the air like a projectile.

The brave youth thought of a trick he would play on his friends. He told the girl, "Lie down and I'll put

<61>

the dead lion on top of you." She lay down and the boy placed the lioness on her.

The young man who had gone in search of water in Naturunku's pit approached the genie's dwelling and said: "*Salaam aleikum.*"

The wife of the genie, who was named Fay Yaz Goni Nya, replied, "Hurry! You'll quiet this baby who has been crying from hunger for three days."

Naturunku's technique was to wring the necks of his victims and then quickly rip off their heads. The genie rushed toward the young man and hit him on the shoulder. The boy pushed Naturunku back until he fell. The genie's wife prayed to God: "Protect us. Since I married Naturunku, I have never seen him have trouble killing a victim, but this trial is proving difficult for him."

The genie stood and jumped on the young man. The latter held him by the belt, and the two tipped left and right, left and right, and then the young man took the genie and threw him in the well where the victims were boiled. The water boiled over the side, then spit the genie out. The young man watched.

<62>

After the water cooled, the boy took some and returned to his friends (the girl and his friend waited for him). They saw him coming, and the one who had killed the lion hurried toward him and said: "Hey! My friend, the lioness has half killed the girl. Look back there. She's devouring her." Since his friend had gone to get the water, they could wash and bury her. The second boy jumped on the lioness and tore at the skin. The boy who had arranged the scene laughed. "Ha! Get up, the lion is already dead." They shook hands in a gesture of friendship.

The third, who had gone to get the fire, arrived at the dwelling of the genie and said, "*Salaam aleikum.*" The genie's wife, Bour-bour Ga Gna, replied, "Hey! Come, we've been waiting for you. We eat ten people every day, but today we're still missing one, so you are welcome."

Maykasumba stood up, ran at the young boy, and hit him on the shoulder. The boy pushed him back until he fell. The genie stood up and leapt at the young man. The latter held him by the belt, tossed him left and right, and right and left. Then he threw

<63>

him in the fire and set his foot on the genie until he burst. The young man let the fire die down, took what he needed, and rejoined his friends who had put the lioness back on the girl and stepped to the side.

"Why are you here?" he asked when he saw them.

"The lioness has killed the girl. See, she's devouring her."

Taking the fire, the third boy jumped at the lioness's body and slashed. The others began to laugh and said, "The lioness is already dead, dear friend. We were just waiting for you."

The girl asked to return home. Back in the village, each boy rejoined his family. "Have you decided?" the girl's relatives asked. "If you take too long, things could go badly. These children would be wise to end their friendship while they all love you."

"That is well, dear parents, but it's a difficult choice. They're all exemplary and courageous. They fought the two genies and the lioness that were keeping us from going to the neighboring village."

The boys' parents presented themselves once more at the house of the girl to find out the choice. The

<64>

girl's family responded that it was difficult, and they must wait patiently as the girl found another way to choose. "Perhaps we'll gather the village to tell of their bravery. That way, everyone can enjoy it."

In the village, there was a large baobab tree that bore only one fruit at the top. The girl asked the three boys to make the fruit fall. The boys went to ask their parents' permission.

Everyone in the village gathered for the occasion. The first suitor went to pick the fruit. He ordered a shoemaker to make him a new pair of shoes. He put the shoes on and climbed the baobab tree until he reached the top. He picked the fruit in front of everyone's eyes, and gave it to the girl. The girl asked him to return it to its place. "*Insha'Allah*," he said. "Ask and it shall be done."

Then it was the second suitor's turn. He prayed for the grace of God and ordered the baobab to bend so the girl could pick the fruit. So it was done, and the girl picked the fruit in front of everyone's eyes. Then she placed the fruit back from where she got it and told the tree to stand again.

<65>

The third suitor went in search of his grandfather's tobacco pipe. He lit the pipe and filled his mouth with smoke that he sent straight up to the fruit so that it fell. The girl collected it, and then the boy returned it to its place. They had all passed the tests. The people of the village asked the girl's family to choose a husband for the girl from among these three boys.

<66>

The Two Bandits

ONE BANDIT WAS Hausa and the other Zarma. The Hausa bandit had collected leaves and grass and put them in a sack. The Zarma bandit in his turn searched for rags and old pagnes to place in his sack. The Hausa bandit said he had tobacco in his sack, the other said he had cotton in his. Everyone was searching for the good-for-nothings. By coincidence, the two met. They exchanged a lengthy greeting and then the Hausa bandit asked the Zarma bandit, "What do you have in your sack?"

"Cotton. What do you have in yours?"

"Tobacco that I would like to sell."

Then, each continued on his way. After a while, they both began to consider, "And if I exchange my

<67>

sack…" and turned back. They met again and traded sacks. Each opened his sack to appraise the merchandise, but alas, discovered he had been tricked by the other. They decided to make their way together. They walked and walked.

A while later they encountered some merchants resting their camels for the night. When the bandits noticed this, one of the two said to the other, "We'll close our eyes and pretend to be blind. Then we'll steal all their goods."

They searched for gum arabic to seal their eyes and for sticks to feel the ground. They walked by the merchants, pretended to trip on them, and said, "*Salaam aleikum.*"

The merchants responded and added, "You're both blind and yet you have no one to guide you?"

"What do you want? It's God who wanted it this way," replied the bandits. "We're going to sleep with you, and you can guide us tomorrow." They took their places next to the merchants.

Ten meters from their bed, there was a pit. After making sure that the merchants had fallen asleep, the

<68>

two bandits got up and took the merchants' things (pagnes and other goods), threw them into the pit, and returned to their beds as if they had done nothing.

When the sun rose, the merchants woke up and realized their belongings were gone. "We've been robbed. Everything's been stolen. We're ruined."

"The blind men stole our things," one of the merchants said. "Beat them."

"It couldn't have been them," said another. "These men cannot see. Look, they're just getting up."

"Fine. Let's leave. There's nothing we can do." They left.

After the merchants had gone, the bandits hurried to the pit to collect the stolen goods.

The Zarma bandit addressed the Hausa bandit. "Since you're from the Hausa region, you should go down into the pit."

"Okay," responded the other, and searched out a vine that would serve as a rope to let him down. The Zarma took each bunch of pagnes that the Hausa passed up to him and ran to hide them, until only one

<69>

was left. The man in the pit wrapped himself up in the fabric.

"The bundle is heavy this time," said the Zarma. "There must be a lot of pagnes." He could hardly get the bundle out of the pit. When he realized that his friend was wrapped up in the pagnes, way before the man revealed himself, the Zarma fled and went in search of the things he had hidden.

The Hausa bandit only retrieved the final bundle. He took it and considered the situation. "That bandit really got me. He took all the pagnes." He returned to the spot where they had committed the robbery and sat. The Zarma bandit also didn't know what to do with his bundles because he couldn't carry them all. He was about to turn around when, suddenly, he heard the cry of a donkey.

"Thank the good Lord! He has given me a form of transport," he said. "I'll go catch it."

The Zarma did not know it was his friend who made the cry. Upon reaching the spot, he pulled the Hausa bandit, who had turned into a donkey, by the ears to his bundles.

<70>

"Let me go," said the Hausa bandit. "I'm not a donkey, I'm your friend. You want to take all the bundles for yourself, but it's not up to you. We must divide them in half."

After dividing them, the Hausa bandit said to the Zarma, "You should give half of your part to me because I'm a merchant. I'll double them, and later you'll come and get them from my house." After their agreement, each went home.

When the day of the rendezvous approached, the Hausa bandit said to his family, "I'm going to die and you'll have to keep me buried me until someone comes to retrieve the things I borrowed from him a long time ago. Perhaps with that trick he'll leave me alone. But fill the grave lightly so I can get out."

The Zarma bandit arrived and asked about his friend.

"He died yesterday, the poor thing," replied the family.

"He died yesterday. He was a true friend."

"Do you need something?"

<71>

"No. I came simply to visit him. I've lost a great friend. Where is his grave? I'm a merchant like him. We did business together."

"His grave is over there."

He prayed at the grave and then returned to the village of the deceased. "I give you my condolences," he said to the family. "I would like to stay here for the night."

When night fell, the Zarma disguised himself as a hyena and went to his friend's grave. He pretended to unearth it, crying like a hyena. The one who was supposedly dead cried out: "Help! The hyena is going to eat me. Help!"

The people ran to help and the Zarma bandit watched until the Hausa was unearthed. Then he appeared and said, "You're dead, right? Why have you come back? Oh, good. Now I get you. You'll reimburse me whether you like it or not." He hit him on the hand and began to laugh.

Those were some great bandits.

<72>

The Farting Girl

IN A VILLAGE there was a very beautiful girl. Her beauty was incomparable. Every time the boys came to her house to chat, she would do nothing but fart until they ran away. But nothing stopped the boys from coming. Soon she had killed twenty boys with her farts. If a boy presented himself there, his relatives knew they needn't prepare a dowry. The family declared that if a boy beat her at a farting contest, she would become his wife without any fanfare.

One day, a young man heard about the girl and prepared himself to go chat. His relatives opposed him. "Would this girl kill a boy she invited to come talk to her?" he asked.

<73>

"You may not go."

The boy refused to obey. He went into the forest and ate some gum arabic. Returning to the village, he bought a calabash of raw peanuts and green beans and asked to have it all boiled. After eating it, he searched for glue to seal his anus, then waited impatiently for night to fall so he could visit the girl. When night fell, he went to her house.

"Salaam aleikum."

Welcoming him, the father and the mother told him that the girl usually chatted outside her hut. He went to the hut, and the girl came out to meet him. She spread a mat, and they sat. The girl did not talk but immediately began to fart: **"Atibuum buum, atibuum buum buut."** After her third volley, the young man reacted. He stood to remove the gum from his anus, and began a bombardment. His fart said, **"Gaddu, gaddu, gadal, ga du, duut."** Both fired off a few rounds of exchanges. The girl was soon exhausted. She died, totally weakened.

<74>

Sana

HERE IS A girl named Sana. She is a very beautiful girl. She wanted to marry someone who had no joints in his body. Every man who came was immediately chased away. One day a snake turned himself into a man to visit her house. He found Sana's mother and stepmother pounding millet in the compound. He greeted them and went straight to Sana's hut. Even before he sat, Sana ran to her mother and said she had found a husband.

"He hasn't even introduced himself and you've already decided," said her mother.

"Yes, mama. He has no joints in his body, so he is the one who will marry me."

<75>

Sana spread out some new mats as an invitation and took a new calabash to serve drinks. She prepared delicious food for her guest. The men returned from the fields, and she went to tell her father about the guest. "Father, I love this man. He will become my husband."

"Since you love him, there's no problem," said her father. "We'll celebrate the marriage."

The young man also said he had come specifically to marry her and take her away.

"Can we celebrate a marriage even though you've come alone?" her father asked.

"It's not a problem. I'm here alone because I rushed my trip and told no one. I would like to celebrate the marriage and leave. One Saturday after, we'll return to pay you a visit."

"Very well. Since you insist, and because you love her and she loves you, too, we'll celebrate the marriage."

The snake paid all the marriage expenses and asked that no one accompany them when they left. He did not want any of the usual formalities. At the

<76>

end of the ceremonies, the newlyweds started their journey to the disguised snake's dwelling. Arriving at a neighboring village to Sana's, he asked her if she knew anyone there. Sana replied yes, that it was the place she went to get leaves to make sauce.

They arrived at another village, and the snake posed the same question.

"This is where we come to find wood," Sana replied.

They went on, passing village after village. Sana had been everywhere. At last, they arrived at their new dwelling. Outside there was a giant tree. The snake sat his wife in the tree and transformed himself. Sana began to cry as she watched the transformation.

"Why are you crying?" asked the snake. "Don't cry. I won't frighten you. I never eat the meat of humans, only that of wild animals."

For ten years, Sana's family heard no news of the married couple. One day, a Fulani encountered Sana while grazing his herds. Surprised, he said, "This is where you've been? Your whole family is worried."

<77>

"Yes! But you must go away quickly. If my husband finds you here, he'll kill you."

She served him a drink and the Fulani shepherd ran to take the news to Sana's family.

"*Salaam aleikum*," said the Fulani.

"*Wa'aleikum as-salaam.*"

"How are you, Sana's mama and papa? I ran into your daughter."

Sana's relatives ordered drinks for the Fulani shepherd because he seemed very thirsty, nearly delirious.

"I am neither hungry nor thirsty," answered the shepherd. "I swear in the name of God that I saw Sana, your daughter."

The parents believed and listened.

"I'll lead those who wish to go to Sana!" said the shepherd.

Of Sana's three older brothers, two decided to accompany the shepherd to find their sister. The other big brother had a handicap: he was leprous. The two brothers ordered the village blacksmith to make them very sharp sabers.

<78>

Not long after, the three men left on their journey. Just before the Fulani shepherd arrived at Sana's house, he gave the signal and they stopped. The two brothers continued until they reached the dwelling where they found Sana. They exchanged a lengthy greeting. Sana begged them to leave, for if her husband found them here, he would kill them.

"We won't leave this place, sister," they said. "Between us, we will kill him."

A moment later, they heard a raucous cry. "What is that?" they asked. "The noise?"

"It's my husband coming home," Sana replied.

"Where was he?"

"He went on a half-day's walk."

"And when he gets here, things'll get worse! Let's get out of here. He mustn't find us here."

The brothers leapt on their horses and rode and rode, so great was their fear. Before they arrived at the village, their shirts were torn. Not far from the village, they got down from their horses and continued on foot. Their fear was great. When they arrived home, they recounted their adventure to their family.

<79>

The leprous brother got up off the ground and said he regretted that the good Lord had punished him. Despite his infirmity, he had decided to go see the blacksmith and ordered him to make a very sharp knife. He asked that the knife be attached to his wrist, and so it was done. The leper looked for a rooster that could serve as a mount to take him to his sister's house. Everyone sang: "*Gorongari ce saw-saw, Gorongari ce saw-saw tamba*," and the rooster began to run. Early in the morning, the man reached his sister's dwelling.

They exchanged a lengthy greeting. "Why have you come here?" asked his sister. "You must stay in the house. You're in grave danger!"

"No, sister. I cannot remain indifferent. I want to hear all your news. I'm dying anyway; don't worry yourself about me. I am not afraid of death. I want your husband to find me here and kill me. I won't budge."

"People who are healthy fled. What can you, a handicapped person, do?"

"Everything will be fine. I want him to find me here."

<80>

He approached the hole where Sana and the snake lived, and waited. A moment later, he heard a raucous noise and asked Sana where it came from.

"It's my husband coming!"

Then the brother approached the hole to wish the snake welcome. "It's true you have no fear," Sana said to him. "I see you're not afraid, but he already knows you're here!"

The snake entered from the other side of the hole, and released some white smoke. After the smoke, he released water droplets. Then he approached his wife and sang to her these words: *"Sana fo, Sana gambay fo."*

And the leper sang back to him, *"Sana fo, Sana gambay fo."*

The snake responded, *"Da ni te ya, kulu ay ga ni ye Sana bande, Sana gambay banda."*

The leper continued to sing. *"Da ni te ya, kulu ay ga ni ye Sana bande, Sana gambay banda, darkan manne, darkan mannari, manne way cabe hair fo, fo Sana."* Then the snake lifted his head from the hole.

<81>

The leper took his knife and cut off the snake's head. Another head appeared, and he cut it off again. Again and again, he cut. A bird circling the scene said to him, "Every time you cut off his head, you must apply the leaves of the sticky grass that the village women use to prepare the sauce for millet." He did so, and the snake fell dead. Immediately, horses, sheep, and cows left the snake's hole. The brother and sister found piles of treasure in the hole, including gold.

After packing up the hoard together, the leper and his sister took the road back home. On the outskirts of the village, they took out all their riches.

The leper hurried ahead and saw that someone had sent word to their parents of their return. The leper arrived home on the back of his rooster.

"My sister, Sana, is on her way with her animals."

Sana's mother took a brand new calabash to serve drinks to her leprous son.

"Come, my son," she said.

"No, mama. I'm not in the habit of drinking water from a new calabash. I'll take my water from where I usually drink with the dogs."

<82>

His mother began to cry.

That is why you should never segregate your own children.

<83>

Notes on the Tales

An excellent source of information on African folklore is Roger D. Abrahams's *African Folktales Selected and Retold by Roger D. Abrahams* (New York: Pantheon Books, 1983).

"The Hyena and the Hare"

This is a tale of greed and unfairness with a moral lesson. Coupled with that is the notion that God (Allah) has a plan. The influence of Islam, now practiced by roughly 80 percent of Niger's population (in both cities and villages), is apparent. The Hyena gracefully accepts his fate, repeating that "God is great." He has faith in Allah, and this is the sort of trust that should be shown by people even when they are in terrible situations.

"The Donkey and the Lion"

This tale introduces the themes of help coming from unexpected places and normally incompatible individuals

<85>

working together. The donkey and the lion represent two types of people. The lion is physically strong, a trait often thought to make a person superior, particularly in a culture dependent on manual labor. The donkey is weaker and, in most circumstances, would succumb to the lion's carnivorousness. The donkey of this tale is clever, and easily tricks the lion into believing he is a hunter. The lion's wife grows suspicious, but the donkey continues to outwit them. In the end, the two skills—intelligence and strength—come together to defeat the hyena.

"The Three Travelers"

This is a pointed tale about keeping a level head and trusting hospitality. The three travelers jump to a (ridiculous) conclusion, and are chastised by their host. Had they thought a moment longer, they would not have destroyed the hut of a kind stranger.

"The Fart Experts"

This tale glorifies the Zarma people, showing them to be superior in skill (in this case, farting) and intellect. The Hausa visitor has the upper hand, but upon the return of the Zarma father, he is frightened away and killed, and the Zarma character receives the prize of the Hausa's fat bull.

"Sanda Wayzayzé"

This is another moral tale. Listeners learn the value of hard work. The lazy villagers are made fools of, while Sanda has a perfect crop and honor from battle. Those who attempt

<86>

to steal what he has worked hard for are humiliated through their fear, while everyone is embarrassed in the end when they realize how they were tricked.

"Betrayal"

This dilemma tale is designed to raise questions of moral values. The story ends by asking the reader to consider the events that came before and come to a decision—in this case, which action represents the greatest betrayal. Tales like this are used to teach about values and focus on the community's rules of social interaction. They also serve to teach skills of argumentation and debate. Often, at the end of such a discussion, a wise elder will weigh in and the group will accede to his assessment.

Elements of the trickster tale crop up in "Betrayal." While common in African folklore, this method is generally unfamiliar to Western readers. According to Lee Haring in "A Characteristic African Folktale Pattern," in *African Folklore*, edited by Richard M. Dorson (Anchor Books, 1972), there are six parts to the trickster tale: false friendship, contract, violation, trickery, deception, and escape. Not all elements need to be present. In this tale, the cycle is repeated several times. The first instance is the meeting between the father and the crocodile. First, the crocodile calls to the man, extending friendship. He then promises not to eat the man or his family, which constitutes a contract. The crocodile violates the contract when he reveals that he wants to eat the man. With the aid of the hare, the man tricks the crocodile into getting out of the water. The crocodile is deceived and travels a kilometer inland.

<87>

The man escapes his death when he places the crocodile on his head and carries him home.

"The Marabout"

This is another trickster tale. It also touches on the important Islamic tradition of the *Hajj*, or pilgrimage to Mecca, which is required at least once in life by those able to afford it. The marabout has traveled a great distance, emphasizing that there is no journey too long to undertake for this purpose. The hyena offers the marabout friendly assistance in exchange for the horse, but then fails to carry through with his agreement. As in "Betrayal," a hare assists the marabout. Once again, the trickster pays for his crime in the end.

"The Election of the Bird King"

This tale advises against making assumptions based on appearances. This is another story in which intelligence is celebrated over strength and size. Judgment should wait until someone has been proven unsuitable for a position. Such discrimination can backfire, as demonstrated when the sasabris defeat each bird sent to destroy them. The value of teamwork is also underscored by this tale; the owl says: "Majesty, the sasabris are stronger than us. They agreed to unite their forces." In village life, working together is vital to guarantee the continuance of the community. In times of war, or attack by other groups, the village is better off presenting a united front than sending only their strongest warriors.

<88>

"The Election of the Animal King"

This tale is set up similarly to "The Election of the Bird King," but the purpose and meaning of the story are different. The turtle changes his appearance for all generations to reflect the sorrow that he feels for the self-sacrifice of the rhinoceros. Unlike the animals that went before him, the rhinoceros knows he will not return and is prepared to die in order to help his fellow animals. The Zarma people honor those who die to defend others.

"The Famine"

This is a lesson in how to maintain a household properly. The father deceives his family so that he might eat well himself. After realizing his family found his bird and collected millet, he demands that they go to the chief, who will determine their punishment. The chief sides with the family, and the father is beaten. The head of the household should share whatever he gains, be it food during a famine or wealth during better times. The wife shows forgiveness, another virtue that increases success in village life, by bringing him millet at the end.

"The Three Heroes"

This courtship tale is another example of a dilemma tale. In this case, the question being raised is one of valor and worthiness. Which of the three young men performed most admirably? The tale also has a secondary purpose. Both male and female listeners learn important lessons about how to behave and what to look for in others. When the characters follow these lessons they are named "exempla-

<89>

ry." The boy's lesson at the beginning can perhaps also give clues as to which values should be considered when answering the tale's question.

"The Two Bandits"

This tale addresses the competition between the Zarma and Hausa people, with the Zarma character coming out on top. Each bandit spends the story using different methods to trick the other into giving up the merchandise. With the final trick, the Hausa man fakes death to escape. The Zarma man proves too clever, and makes fun of the Hausa man for trying. In Niger, the Hausa are known as the businesspeople, while the Zarma are pastoral. Here, the Zarma show that they can be just as savvy as the Hausa when it comes to money.

"The Farting Girl"

This tale seems at first to be nothing more than a humorous tale. However, it is also a tale of courtship and a picture of male-female relations in Zarma culture. It starts, unusually, with a woman taking a leading role. There are few cases in African culture in which a woman shows autonomy. The girl in the story refuses to marry unless beaten at a farting contest. That her parents allow this gives a glimpse into the family dynamic—marriages are not arranged without the woman's consent. In the end, the woman's place below the man in the social hierarchy is underscored by the boy winning the contest. Furthermore, women should not be too picky, or they will never get married at all!

<90>

"Sana"

> This tale is, in the end, a story with a moral. It is another
> example of a woman setting the conditions for whom she
> will marry (he must have no joints). Things quickly go
> downhill for Sana when she discovers the true nature of her
> husband, which reflects the culture in which women are
> subordinate to men. Two of Sana's brothers and the Fulani
> shepherd go to try and rescue her, but flee in fear. The
> action up to this point has been nothing more than set-up
> to introduce the hero, Sana's leprous brother. He bravely
> rescues Sana from her husband and they return home,
> laden with treasure. Now we discover that he has been mis-
> treated throughout his life because of his leprosy. His
> mother is upset when he refuses better treatment now that
> he has achieved a great feat. As with many African moral
> tales, the moral is stated clearly at the end.

<91>

Glossary

baobab A distinctive looking tree with a tall, thick trunk and a wide umbrella of branches. The leaves are edible, but it is better known for its fruit, also known as "monkey bread." The fruit is large and ovular with a hard shell. The meat inside is dry and powdery. It is also ground into powder to make a popular beverage.

calabash Round gourds that are dried and sometimes decorated to make bowls and other containers, as well as drum like instruments. They vary in size and shape.

compound A walled off area within a village in which a family group has their huts and keeps their livestock.

exodus During the dry season, men travel to the coast to find work and make money.

<93>

Fulani A semi-nomadic people who move across the land with their herds.

griot A musician, usually hired to play at weddings and other celebrations.

Hausa The largest ethnic group in West Africa. Most, even in small villages, practice the Muslim faith.

Insha'Allah An Arabic phrase meaning "God willing."

kora A 21-string guitar made from a calabash and used traditionally in West African cultures.

lengthy greeting In many African cultures, greetings are long, ritualistic exchanges of statements and responses.

maï-biddiga A gun carrier.

marabout A Muslim teacher of the Qu'ran.

millet The cereal grain millet is the main crop of Niger. The head of the millet is called an ear. The grains are removed and pounded by women in large, deep mortars to break them down for the preparation of food.

millet ball A fried ball of ground millet.

muezzin In Islam, the man appointed to call the people to prayer.

<94>

pagne A piece of material, often brightly colored. It may be used for many purposes, including as a wrap-around skirt, a towel, a sheet or a wrap for tying a baby to one's back.

rainy season When the rains fall, from June to September. Millet is planted and grown at this time. Annual rainfall ranges between nine and thirty centimeters. The rest of the year is dry and hot.

salaam aleikum/wa'aleikum as-salaam A traditional Muslim greeting and reply meaning "Peace be upon you" and "Upon you be peace."

Wallahi "I swear to Allah that it's the truth." Used as a confirmation of the truth or as an Arabic exclamation of shock or disbelief.

Zarma A branch of the Songhay people of West Africa. They are localized around Niamey, the capital of Niger, and live along the Niger River. They are mostly farmers. They also practice the Muslim faith.

<95>